Madame Two Swords

Madame Two Swords

Tanith Lee

Stafford England

Madame Two Swords
By Tanith Lee
© 1988, 2nd edition 2017

Cover art by Ruby
Interior illustrations by Jarod Mills, except for decorations on pages 85 and 107 by Storm Constantine
Interior layout by Storm Constantine

Set in Palatino Linotype

ISBN 978-1-907737-81-7

IP0133

An Immanion Press Edition
http://www.immanion–press.com
info@immanion–press.com

Tanith Lee

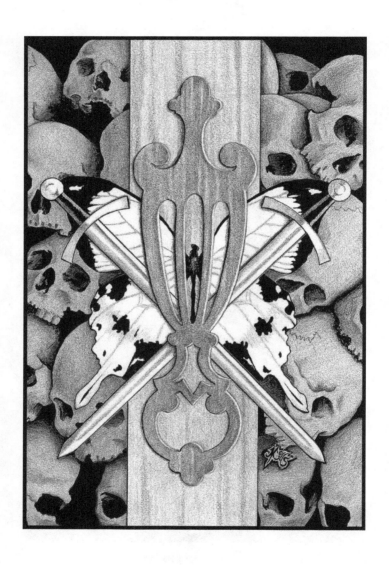

ONE

The day the terrible old woman first looked at me, with those black eyes like swords, I had been to a funeral. It was my mother's. I was the only mourner.

I had not been able to pay the priest very much, and he gabbled the words. It was a chilly spring afternoon of tarnished sunlight, and he was anxious to get back indoors. The wind whipped his dingy *soutane*, and he stared at the book and read fast through pinched lips. Besides, I had been to church rarely, and did not know any of the forms – when to kneel, when to join in the prayer, or whether to keep silent. I sensed he despised me and despised my mother's corpse, too, perhaps, for daring to come here for burial in this irreligious condition; the state system of crematoria did very well for such people as we. But then my father and mother had bought this plot between them years ago, when they had been happy, I suppose, and death something like a small dark hill just beginning to crest the horizon ahead of them.

Twenty paces away, another funeral was going on and on, the clothes of mourners trembling in the wind like huge charred leaves. And somehow then I remembered Lucien's burying two hundred years in the past, the tipping of bodies and heads into one gaping hole, by the ravenous light of torches, which showed everything, under the thin rain. Nearby, the rabble, that small portion which was not yet too tired, too sated, too drunk to care, stood jeering, still mocking the carcasses that had no longer the wit to react. And the rabble of foreign soldiery, leaning on muskets or swords, smoking and drinking, or eating sausages. And beyond these, the women, those brave or foolish enough to have come. Slender, shadowy, veiled, they stood about in little groups, like sisters, or the chorus in a Greek tragedy. Some of them wept. Some were silent. Either way, it scarcely mattered anymore.

The priest closed his prayer-book with a snap. The cold dry daylight wind sliced between us.

"Thank you," I said.

He took the coin from my gloved hand and nodded to me unsmilingly. He strode off in his flapping robe, leaving me alone above my mother's grave.

I looked down into the opened ground. I was not certain what to do. I did not shed any tears; that was long over. She had been ill so many weeks, and I had known all along this would be the end. Twenty paces away, the black clothes still fluttered and the priest still droned. I felt ashamed, awkward, lingering there with my insignificant grief. So I turned and wandered between the immaculate graves, out into the city, where cars hooted, and people laughed and argued in front of the restaurants. As I stepped through the gate, birds scattered like brown and white crumbs along the boulevard. I was not the reason. A large old-fashioned carriage was trundling by, drawn by horses. Involuntarily, I hesitated, just in the same way that the birds flew; the conveyance seemed bigger than it was, and to overlap the pavement with its side. There was some faded lettering there, done in yellow and green. It reminded me incoherently of circuses, exhibitions... My only clear impression was of two swords, crossed just under the hilts, and that this symbol started my heart into a momentary uneven rhythm, although I did not know why. The horses, the driver, were already past, and then a window of the carriage came level. Out of darkness there evolved a narrow pale shape, a face peering out. Its eyes were directly on me, as if I had been expected to be exactly where I was. The image I received was of a face so old, so worn and fined and torn by age, that it was hardly more than tissue paper over dark bone. The eyes, though, were quite terribly vital and alive. So black and wetly clear, so penetrating I seemed to have been stabbed by them. I recoiled, perhaps even physically, and then the carriage was past, was going away.

I felt an emotion I could put no name to, although the tumult of it shook me. Almost instantly I assigned appropriate descriptions: embarrassment, even superstition. They could only, after all, be a bad omen, those savage black eyes of a tortured young girl staring into mine from that mummy's face.

I tried to thrust the picture from my mind, and so it was not for almost another hour that I remembered where I had seen the carriage-marking of the swords before.

I had found myself seated outside a café, among that wheel of streets that leads to all points of the compass from the hub of the cenotaph. The trees in their wire baskets were touched with luminous dabs of blossom, which the wind blew on to the pavements, in places so thickly it looked like fresh snow. I had ordered coffee, because I could afford nothing else. My gloves were darned. I felt constrained in my black coat with its little bit of fur around the collar, my black bell-hat, as if I had carried the poverty-stricken funeral away with me and had no business to be sitting here with normal people.

There had been nothing grand or noble or even particularly sad in what had happened.

Presently, I found I had opened my purse and taken out of it the little clothbound book.

I drew off my gloves so that I could make a more immediate contact between the surface and my own flesh. Poor little book, cracked and stained from being carried everywhere and in all manner of vehicles – pockets, sashes, purses – from being read in the hot sun or the cold winter, or in the rain with the drops falling on the pages suggesting tears. And here was the dark stain from when some girl at the academy had spilled ink maliciously across my desk, and a spot of red wine from some long-ago supper, when there were coloured lamps hung up in the trees, and the boy I wanted to dance with me had danced only with others, and I had held the book in my hands against my stiff new cheap frock – and a bottle had been spilled suddenly at the next table...

The book was my talisman. Other girls wore crosses or medallions.

When I was fourteen, I used occasionally to go to second-hand bookshops in the *Vieux Quartier* of Troy, where most things were inexpensive and generally of 'slight' use. My mother did not really like me to go to the Old Quarter, so it was a sort of adventure. Nothing ever happened to me; perhaps I wished it would. I was fat then, though maybe not so fat as I thought; my hair was dingy because we never bought shampoo, and had to make do with hard embittered lumps of kitchen soap, which also made my skin so blotchy that some days I would cry about it. In those years, I seemed alone in my infirmities. I began to dread myself as if I were some disease I had caught. It was a day in late autumn when I went into the bookshop. Like all of old Troy it was airless, overhung and concealing. My mother had given me some money to buy stockings, since the darning in the existent pair had started to resemble extraordinary embroidery. But I did not of course like buying stockings. The narrow-hipped assistants undermined me, and I had put it off.

The man in the shop took no notice of me; I was not a good customer since I plainly had no means to buy anything. But I was timid, would cause no trouble. He left me to rummage among the magazines, the torrid novels, and the dry travelogues with their blurred etchings of wrecked temples and aqueducts. My book was lying between the pages of one of these, I forget which, as if it had taken up hiding there. Later I wondered who could have possessed such a thing; what in the world had driven them to let it go. The blue cloth binding was quite pristine under its dust. It was a slender book, without lettering. I opened it out of curiosity.

There are only five pieces in the volume, the long prose epic the 'Philosophy of the *Droits*', and the supporting articles before and after the storming of La Tour, and two fragments of the greater poems, the 'Call to Arms', and the 'Night Song', which became an epitaph. I would guess that some of his work, the prose at least, had already been rehearsed at the academy. But the fierceness and the passion were expurgated, and to one not naturally inclined, the politics are complex and the intrigue far from easy to understand. For the poetry – I seemed to comprehend what he wrote only by letting it wash over me in a vast wave, knowing it by my heart and my inner eyes. To try to analyse the stanzas was to let them slip from the grasp like fine sand.

However, it was not the poetry or the politics that first jolted me awake in that drab little shop. It was the painting, the wonderful small water-colour which somebody had left lying there between the flyleaf and the cover, as if they had meant it for me, meant for me to find it. It would have fetched a good price, I expect, but I did not know it then and resolutely, through all the years of our poverty which followed, I for ever refused to know it. After all, perhaps it was, though hand-done, only a copy. In any case, I would rather have sold my eyes or my hands for bread than that cameo on paper, which contained his face.

I suppose that when one is fourteen and trapped by one's own immaturity, unleavened, undirected, let for all that poised on the threshold of readiness, of *need*, longing, or some form of blind desire, (and I do not necessarily mean sexual desire), must occur. It is the only way to find beauty or adventure, and they are the universal dreams of mankind; beauty and adventure, and love.

In the painting, his face is long and dark, darker than in reality, I think, for the portrait appears to have been worked on when the candle flame was burning low. The hair and brows are black, and the eyes of a very definite almost elongated shape, wide-set, and in that curious blank look of thought which the artist has caught in them you can see how the eyelid of the left eye is a fraction wider than the other, a detail which at other times would be invisible. The colour of the eyes, too, is dark. His looks are concentrated, condensed even, vivid. And there is an energy that seems about to spring from the paper. It was hard to imagine being able to stand such an implicit barrage for long, like too-strong sunlight in the eyes – you would want to look at something plain or apathetic to relieve them. But at the same time, there is a sort of twisting about the mouth, something not entirely physical, but that can eventually be made out in every part of the countenance.

At fourteen, I did not really notice any of this. Only the face. And I burned, a sort of blush, a sort of fire, as if I had actually looked into his eyes across the two hundred years between us; as if he stood there in front of me.

I bought the book with my mother's money. And then, stumbling and confused, I wandered out of the shop by a side entrance, which I think had been left open for a carter to come in and out, for one passed me. To the rear was a cobbled yard, with craning upper storeys glowering down on it. An alley, just wide enough for carts, went under them to the street. Exactly opposite was an old stables with closed doors, and above a long floor with shuttered windows. Along this floor a black-painted board had been fixed, showing two crossed swords in yellow and bright green, and under these the English words: *Two Swords*, unnecessarily. Just that, nothing else.

I had stopped, bewildered by my mistaken exit, then somehow taken aback by the curious sign, and a strange sensation that seemed to emanate from it. The shuttered windows, indeed, everything about the stables and the second storey, gave signs of absolute unlife. Perhaps the owner of the bizarre sign had moved away.

Just then the carter came by me again, empty handed.

"Thinking of calling on Madame? Don't do it. That's a bad lot up there. A creepy old side-show not fit for a young girl. Tarot. Things like that. And death-masks. And musical boxes made from skulls. And she, the old witch. She's a hundred if she's a day."

I was aware he was trying to frighten me, and I did not like his looks. The man in the shop called to him, and as he turned I ran away, holding to me, as I ran, the book.

So it was I saw the two swords, for the first, that very afternoon I found the book of fragments and the portrait of Lucien de Ceppays.

I read the articles, the exhortations, the poems, not understanding them, loving them because they were his, in the public gardens where the leaves blew crisply bronze and yellow round my feet. At dusk, I went home in a dream, expecting martyrdom for my purchase, but my mother had forgotten about the stockings. My father, on the way home from the little tailors where he worked, had collapsed in the street. Neighbours had helped him to the house, and three days later he was dead.

…the man in the shop took no notice of me…

TWO

The night after my mother's funeral, the sun died violently. Evening rose like a tide behind the towers of the old cathedral, which have dominated Troy ever since the city was the market-town of Trois, seven hundred years ago. I had been home to the *Rue St. Marc* to change my frock and coat and my shoes. My landlady stood in her doorway and watched me go up the stairs and come down them. There was a greasy handprint on the door of my closet, where she had poked about among my things while I was out, but I had nothing of value for her to take, though once or twice, during my mother's illness, the landlady had come to visit her and afterwards a little sugar or coffee might be missing, and once some oranges. She did not see this as stealing, but as a sort of payment in kind against the day when she knew we would fall seriously behind with her rent. That day had now, of course, arrived.

When I went downstairs again, she called out to me: "Poor Madame's funeral went off well? I don't want to trouble you, naturally, at such a time, but there has been nothing paid now for three weeks."

"I hope to be able to pay you tomorrow," I said. It was not true, which she understood.

She said, "I don't think you can say, Mademoiselle, that I've been uncharitable."

"No, you've been very good. I shall speak to my employer tonight at the café, ask him for an advance. Then I can settle with you."

She smiled archly. The smile said what I did to get the money was all one to her. I think she told people I was a prostitute, because sometimes when I went down to buy milk, and passed our neighbours, they drew aside and looked me up and down in the particular way one sort of woman has for another sort. However, I was only a waitress at the *Café Silver*, and not pretty enough to attract much attention, except sometimes at the dimmer tables, from older men. They would put their hand on you and ask you a question very low, which had a double meaning, and their teeth were always bad, and their flesh was like white jelly. It was possibly foolish to refuse their advances, they might have been persuaded to pay well.

But I was a virgin, quite inexperienced, and besides I was afraid of their dirtiness. It seemed to me I was always trying to remain clean, to bathe every day in a few inches of warmed water, to wash my clothes and everything that I came into contact with – sheets, curtains, the grey porcelain sink, and the dull implacable windows of the room where my mother died. In any case, I had been enchanted by a man very young. Though I had sometimes seen other men I had wanted, it was only because in some way they resembled him. Three or four times a boy had caught my hand, caressed my cheek, and twice young men had taken me for supper at a little restaurant, and walked with me by the river near midnight, when all the clocks in Troy seem to chime together, and kissed me with hunger. But these brief excursions into intimacy had faltered on some deep iron rock inside myself – I was cold, or frigid, or else they did not know what I was thinking, or I was too serious, or I would not let them make love to me. I was terrified of becoming pregnant, and no one advised me, I had no notion where I should go for advice. But more than this, I could not give myself because their demands, their laughter, the touch of their hands, did not seem real. At least, not as real as that paper face I carried in my brain. I was no longer fat. My skin was clear and firm, as long as I did not try to use rouge or powder like the other girls at the cafe, when it would break out in a rash. On the twilit pavements in my high-heels, a man might turn and look at me, but never under a lighted lamp. I was too plain to make my own terms, and would not live by any others.

When I had left my landlady and gone out into the street, all the windows were softly lit against the dusk.

The wide boulevards rang with neons and shouted music. The Franco-English city, which now speaks the mix known sneeringly as *Frenish*, aside from its own patois, never seems more polyglottal than after dark. Though it is always vituperative.

I came to the cafe and went in and down the narrow stairway, and presently knocked on the maroon door. For the first week of my mother's illness, I had managed to work in the afternoons, and my employer had given me half-pay, but soon I could no longer leave her and then the money had stopped. The door opened suddenly, and there he stood, Monsieur

Sandarac in his white suit and spotted tie, his little eyes cautiously not recognising me.

"Good evening, Monsieur. I have come to ask you for my job back."

"Job? Back?" He wrinkled his upper lip, a sort of smile, but in a monkey a sign of warning. "Ah, yes. I remember you." He ushered me in, followed me, and sat in the only chair. A bottle of red wine and a half-filled glass stood on the table; he looked at it thoughtfully. "You left, if I recall, to nurse your mother. Better, I trust?"

"No, monsieur. My mother died a few days ago. That is why I'm free to work again."

He sucked at his teeth.

"Well, I've had to fill your place, you know."

I had expected nothing else.

I said, "Do you have any other vacancies?"

"Vacancies?" he asked the glass in surprise.

"Such as washing dishes, sweeping the floor."

"It's hard to get work in the city. Don't I know. When I advertised your job, you should have seen the girls out on the pave-ment. And some of them willing to do more than wait table. I've been good to you, *petite*, I kept you on even when I had a complaint or two -- you have to jolly the patrons along, you know. Make sure they have a good time."

"I see," I said. I turned towards the door.

"You should try the laundries," he said. "They can usually take a girl on. Or go to the coast, there's work there, once the season starts. But then, I don't suppose you have the train fare for the coast. The laundries, then. Naturally," he said, "if you were willing…"

"What?"

"No," he said, smiling all his sucked teeth at me in triumph. "I won't suggest it. Better try it your way, eh, *petite*?"

He waited for me to beg him to let me go upstairs with some special, not-too-particular friend of his.

I had left the academy when I was fifteen, and I had no qualifications; I had had to take whatever work I could after my father's death, and it taught me nothing, only the futility of pride and obstinacy. So I almost blurted out I would do whatever Monsieur Sandarac wished, only give me a trial. But the words refused to come. I looked at him, and then turned and walked out of the maroon office, up the narrow stair, into the gaudy neon night. And I heard him shout behind me:

"Do as you like then, Mademoiselle, and don't come snivelling to me when your guts are stuck on your backbone, you pot-faced bitch."

I was afraid to return to my rooms at once, for then my landlady would know I had not regained my job and the rent would not be paid.

In the gardens where I walked, lovers were walking also, their hands intimately knotted. The moon rose like a cold stone.

I thought of the old woman, her face like the moon's, but pierced by those swords of starving desperate eyes. Yes, she had looked at me. What had she wanted? For she had wanted something.

After midnight, it was safe to go home.

Home. Upstairs, the dingy two rooms. I could keep them clean, but not make them brighter, despite the frantic touches of colour I had introduced – a bunch of flowers in a jar, or a dish of small red plaster fruits, the cracked shell mirror before the window, my black lacquer box with the crimson dragons, and the lamp with its bowl-topped shade, decorated with yellow glass in the shapes of crocuses. That lamp, rescued at a curb-side auction two years ago, was my prize.

I lit my lamp. I was too tired to eat. Just as well, there was only a little bread and some bruised apricots. These would do for tomorrow.

I sat and opened the cloth book, and began to read the *Summation Aux Armes*. Though in pure French, it was dotted by pieces of Shakespeare, Plato, Truvius. The long winter of discontent must pass, spring, the green leaf of hope, the swelling bud, spring would break open her bonds. The earth would shudder and crack, throwing off the burden of snow, heavy and white, that froze men's hearts. Spring was on the march, a mighty river in spate. It would seize and sweep away anything that stood in its path.

And *Spring is on the march!* the crowd shouted. The wretched crowd, empty of food, denied all help, with only hope and spirit to feed it and keep it alive. So it was not hard to rouse them, as he stood shouting to them under the trees, and he clearly felt the power of it, he too caught up in their drunkenness – his passionate wish to see their state alleviated, the conviction that it would be possible to make them move, like some colossal galvanic engine, and he the spark which fired it. "A river – a river – sweep tyranny and injustice away!" the crowd screamed. "To arms! To arms!" And rushing like this river in spate through the streets, it found arms for itself, swords, sticks, muskets, paving stones. Lucien de Ceppays' address to the people ultimately ended at eleven o'clock that night in the storming of the great prison of La Tour – the Tower, or *Tour*

Mort – Death Tower, as it was sometimes known. Here those prisoners moped who had been shut away without trial at a whim of the monarchy or nobility. It was a symbol. And in the black hour of eleven, the sky above Troy burned bloody-red with the fires of exploding cannon, as La Tour collapsed in rubble.

So the march had begun, the Spring March. Unstoppable, once started. One by one, the winter trees were cut down, the rotted elm of a king, the clinging cherry of a queen; as fast and plenteous as leaves, a world of persons fell. And then another cry: Whatever *stands* – falls.

All this while, Lucien, at the forefront of the tumult, the poet of the Revolution, whose stanzas became songs, and whose witty caricatures were hung about the necks of those who were themselves hanged from the lamp-poles of the city, or pinned to the backs of those whose heads were struck from the body with a honed sword.

On the borders, meanwhile, war was everywhere raging, as from all sides the monarchies of other kingdoms took fright. England, Allemagne, La Suisse, striving to cauterise the running wound of social change, the rushing torrent, that might infect their own masses with revolt.

Disorganised from within, stupefied by

blood, a rampaging heart without a brain, France staggered and then crumbled before the onslaught.

Again, red skies over Troy, but not from the pyre of injustice. Death assumed new forms. She sat in the citadel with a pale stern face. England, the old enemy, had taken back the wild thing, France, into her custody. The new government which was then set up had the shape of English law and English desires, of English puppet-masters. It ended in chains then, the march to liberty, the cry of brotherhood. And for Lucien de Ceppays and his confreres, the *danse macabre* had come full circle. English law had also imported a new machine of death, a blade that worked almost by itself, and was less exhausting, therefore, for the executioner, poor fellow, with so much work on his hands. Doctor Guyot's invention: *La Guyotine*. (Circuses for the rabble, if not bread.)

Those who live by the sword really do die by a sword, so the *Chanson Nuit* exclaims. "But so many candles are to be snuffed out, it will be a dark night, this one."

The last poem was smuggled from the prison. It came into the hands of Lucien's mistress, Camélie.

Of Camélie the books know little. A

mysterious shadowy figure, she haunts the burial ground with the others, finally emerging among the rabble, the English soldiers, with her long cry like the hooting of an owl – *Vive la Revolution revolu!* But the torch-lit caves of dungeons did not hold her long. She was spared death, although it would seem she had demanded death as her right. She returned instead into the mysterious shadows. And Troy of the *Marche Printemps*, the Revolution, the invading army and the clashing downstroke of *La Guyotine*, and of, once more, poverty and hopelessness, of the independence of puppets, of *Frenish*, decaying apricots, a scrap of bread, two hundred years of Troy went on.

A moth fell against my lamp in its own ecstasy of death. I blew out the flame. Tomorrow I must walk from café to café, asking after work, without much optimism. Perhaps a girl might have fallen sick, if I were lucky and she not. Otherwise, there was the southern sector of the city with its factories, those hells of black air and noise, in which the eardrums failed after one year, and north the white hells of the laundries of the *Rue George*. I had seen the women come from the laundries. The wonderful chemical cleansers in the vats mottled their hands like the plucked corpses of chickens; their eyes were affected often, and always they coughed. But I was strong. Perhaps I could last eighteen months, and meanwhile find someone and pay them to teach me fine sewing, or pottery. Skills were at a premium in Troy, rare, and work much rarer.

I lay in the dark room on my bed, the clothbound book under my pillow, as it had always been, first put there with romance, later as a comfort, an amulet. Though politics were alien to me, the passion, the rage – yes, certainly I had for some years understood these. I, back bowed, trodden into the rainy gutter, with so many like me.

I could not sleep for a long while. I had grown used to the breathing of my mother and used to rising in the night to help her or bring her medicine. She had not lived long, and I remembered the face of the old woman in the old-fashioned carriage, who had surely abused her span. ("Madame – old witch – a hundred if she's a day.") A hundred? She had looked it.

But it was unwise to think of her. I would soon grow accustomed to being alone.

THREE

The apricots tasted of sawdust, but I ate them carefully, making them last.

Then I put on my black 'respectable' coat and my *cloche* hat, and went out and down the street. A cold pink bloom still lingered in the east, and a man went by with a wagon selling milk.

Most of the *cafés-nuits-blanches* are closed by day, but 1 knocked at each, went up metal stairways or down wooden ones, and stood among stacked-up tables, or against walls where posters peeled like damaged skin. Sometimes, I would try a little shop, a tobacconist's or a raddled boutique. Noon came, and I had not been lucky. The city seemed all one amalgamated face and one voice, saying *Allez*, saying *Rien*; saying *No*. I stood under some trees and counted the coins in my purse. A car hooted at me and flashed by, shining in the thin sun – even sunlight owed it service. There are always some who can afford those things we cannot.

I decided I had better not buy coffee, only a glass of water, which was cheaper. If I drank the water slowly, it would dull the empty ache in my stomach, and then I should be able to go up to the *Rue George*. Through the dirty north window of the restaurant, I could see the grey-white steam of the laundries rising in irregular clots above the streets. I think I took out my book and pressed it together in my hands, but the waiters were anxious I should go. Presently, I had finished the glass of water, rose, and began to walk slowly northwards.

There was as usual a great cluster of women in the square yard that opened directly on the pavement. They had an appearance of exhausted malevolent birds, in their overalls and the cloths that bound their hair. All the mottled hands were busy, with knitting or cards, as they squatted on benches, or rolling small tubes of tobacco; the jaws, too, were working with gum or cheap sweets. Not many were talking, only the huge chimneys belched and hissed behind them. The air was raw with the smell of damp material, sweat and chemicals.

I was afraid to go into the yard. Already they had stiffened at my presence, scenting me, seeming prepared to peck or scratch as I went by. But I meant to be one of them. These were my sisters. I made myself move forward and took a few steps across the paving. All at once, the crowd parted and a woman came through and straight up to me.

She stared at me with her bleached-out eyes, her red and purple hands thrust in the pockets of a long shapeless coat. She was older than me but not much, about twenty-four or five, but tough and entirely menacing.

"What do you want, miss?"

"I'm looking for work," I said

"Work, eh?" She looked round, and the crowd murmured throatily. "You look to me like you could get work doing other things. You've had schooling, haven't you?" she accused. She reached out and plucked at the scrap of fur around my neck. "Some gentleman buy you that? Some *très beau monsieur*? Go on, girlie. You go and find something else."

"I haven't any money." I tried to talk reasonably, not to give offence or incite her further. "I owe three weeks' rent."

"Rent?" She smiled, and around us the sea of women pressed closer. "So you have a nice room to pay rent on. You should live like me, missie, with the rats. They suck the blood out of the legs of your babies, they do, but they don't ask for any rent, eh, girls?" She looked into my face, deep into it. She saw my physical softness, and my fear. "My sister's laid up," she said, "but tomorrow she'll be better. You come here and ask and they'll give you her job, won't they, and then Christ knows what my sister will do. No, you take yourself off, miss, and find some kind gentlemen to look after you again, and don't come trying to steal the work from us that slave and cough up our lungs to keep your dirty sheets clean, and your dresses pretty for when he takes you to a naughty show. Go on." She pushed me, not particularly hard, and suddenly a woman on my left spat on my coat.

A dreadful panic of tears came up behind my eyes, and the water I had drunk rushed back into my throat. I was not brave and could summon up no arguments or deeds. I took a step backwards.

"That's it," she said to me. Her eyes were half-blind, but terrible as those of basilisks. "And don't bother trying any other door in the street. There are ten laundries, and there's someone like me in every one of them."

I turned, and the other women hemmed me in. Their sweet gum-breath struck my nostrils and nearly made me retch.

The rabble – *la canaille* – yes, a female thing. Yet changeless. Men change, times change, the Rabble – never. One great hoarse voice whining and shrieking in its pain, crying out like something wounded under a wheel. Crying for pain, for blood, to be visited on all others. And in its fear, turning always to rend, even, the hand that reaches out to aid.

He found that, did he not? The way the rabble will turn, its yellow teeth bared. The beast which leaps for the throat of the fallen master at the order of the new master whose hand now twitches the leash...

Such a mob, indeed any crowd, had always frightened me.

I pushed through them in wild terror and fled on to the pavement. The gob of spit was drying on my coat. The cold sweat ran down my back. I walked rigidly away. They did not call after me.

I sat, too debilitated to move about, for some hours in the museum in the *Quartier Grèche*.

It is very quiet in the museum in the afternoon; not many people come there now to look at the pictures, black armour and broken urns. Seven years ago, just before I left the academy, I would sometimes come there. There were books that might be read, though not taken away. I read something about Lucien – that is how I learned the outline of his life – and his poetry, which was easier come by, and such pamphlets of his as existed under glass, some with most macabrely ironic headings, such as *The Debate Between The Gallows and The Aristocrat, (Which Can Only End One Way: Hanging In The Air)*.

Today the sunlight shafted down from the high windows on the cases of papers and gems, powdered like the wings of butterflies with an ethereal gilded dust. Then the light reddened. I got up, like a somnambulist, and set off for my rooms. I was so tired I felt I must sleep long and deeply. Perhaps, while I slept, something might happen, some alteration in my fortunes, or the world.

When I had turned into the *Rue St. Marc*, the street was in shadow and the lamp-lighter far off yet, moving at a slow pace with his glow-worm trail of fire. As I reached the dismal steps of home, I noticed a little lacquer box decorated with dragons left out on the pavement, and did not immediately recognise it as mine. But I came closer and saw sticking up from it my hair-brush like a balding porcupine, and certain articles of clothing, my paper books, and the cracked shell mirror... 'Home', it seemed, was 'home' no longer.

I felt no surprise or shock, only stood by the stone balustrade and stared about me with a vague disorientated numbness. Presumably, the landlady had been watching for me, however, because her window opened, with no light behind, and she spoke down at me with a bland sort of menace.

"That's all your bits there. Except a few things of mine, and a trifle or two your mother gave me, perhaps without you knowing. In lieu of the rent."

I stood there and looked at her. She would have kept the lamp with the crocuses; she had always had a fancy for that. I was going to lie that there would be money in the morning, someone would bring it, but she forestalled me.

"Now you won't expect me to believe any silly tales, will you? I can always find someone willing to pay good cash for your room, and no more 'I'll have it tomorrow,' if you please. I am sure, if you can get employment, I'll consider taking you back. But we all have to live, mademoiselle."

Where I had been stone cold I was suddenly hot. I had intended nothing, but my voice came out of me, strong and ringing, like a shout. "You'll be rich then, Madame, battening on the poor. That is the way, isn't it? Dog eat dog. I've seen nothing else all day. But what of the wolves, Madame, feeding on us both. Think, Madame, *think* what you're doing. No, I don't care about your thefts, but your stupidity – that is despicable. Hang a veil over your mirror, so you needn't look yourself in the face!"

She balanced above me, astonished, her mouth open. Then she backed away, the window slammed. I, too, was quite astonished and did nothing. I stood and watched in a daze as her curtains were drawn and warm light at last rose behind them. Maybe, the light of the crocus lamp.

I felt weak, as if an electric current had passed through me and then died. I leaned on the balustrade for a minute, until I felt I could move.

Then I took up the lacquer box. She had not packed my second coat into it; she would no doubt sell the coat in the market. The box, missing so much that was rightfully its own, was not very heavy.

I walked towards the river.

At one time, it was fashionable to drown in the river, even fashionable to be saved from drowning in it.

I sat down at last on a bench under the chestnut trees, close to *Trois Filles* Bridge. The old pylons of the bridge sank into the river.

How many times had Lucien travelled over the bridge? Once, at least, in that cart daubed in scarlet and blue, drawn by the horses decked in coloured ribbons. Those in power had made the progress like a carnival – which indeed it was, carnival – *carne vale* – having the meaning *farewell to the flesh*. The *Place de la Mort* lay over that way, up on a hill – as Lucien had said, a new journey to an old Calvary.

As the cart rattled over the river, the whole city had seethed. Accused of deluding the people, leading them into war and so into defeat, the party *en route to La Guyotine* had been reviled and jeered. Things had been flung at the cart and into it. (On the house doors of those due to die had been scrawled, in the blood of butchered pigs, the word TRAITOR, over and over, with other epithets.) But flowers fell in the cart as well as eggs. And a woman in the crowd shouted, "You will make a pretty corpse, Monsieur Ceppays."

They say he called back, "Though you paint an inch thick, lady, someday so will you."

He had a way with words. Words had helped him up the ladder of the scaffold.

But I stopped thinking even of this, as I sat by the river under Three Girls Bridge. There was the smell of spring rain sweet on the air, a thin moon like paper, through which one seemed to see the backdrop of sky, torn sails of clouds above the cathedral on its island. And below in the water, the reflected lamps. In other words, I was surrounded by *life*.

I did not hear or see the man approach. He came and sat beside me and was suddenly there.

"You are in some trouble?" he said softly.

I did not look at him.

"Not at all."

"Oh yes. You are in some bad trouble."

His voice was not musical, but quite gentle, with a note of restraint. My heart had begun to thud, the beats seeming too large for my body.

"Tell me, what would you do for this?" And from the corner of my eye I glimpsed the bill in his hand.

"What would you want me to do?"

"What do you think?"

Dog feeding on dog. While the wolves laugh from their safe high walls.

I could not make myself look at him. Every bone and tendon in my body had congealed in an uncontrollable rigor.

"Very well."

Despite the rigor, I got to my feet. A curious sensation, my back was steel, my legs water. He also rose, and I realised at once he must be deformed, some sort of dwarf. He took my elbow politely. We walked slowly along the bank.

I began to notice things. He seemed clean. There were the callouses of a machine-worker on his hands. His shoes, marked in places by acid burns, were yet otherwise highly and carefully polished. But I did not want to know these things, or anything about him. He would give me money. My mind said to me: *Why not?* But my flesh quaked.

Presently, we ascended steps and turned aside into a cobbled street. Bright light flooded out like spillings from the cafés. Now I should say to him, buy me food, first. But the thought of food, even the smell of it, sickened me. When he asked me, as he abruptly, quietly, did, if I would like something to drink – chocolate, coffee, a *fine* perhaps, or *anisette* – I shook my head. I carried my box in one arm, which ached now. My whole body ached. We seemed to go on and on. Where was he taking me?

The gas popped in the street-lamps. There seemed fewer of them. Men had been hanged from the lamp-poles of the city, once. I realised we had moved into the Old Quarter of Troy, and my escort must have felt my hesitation. He said, quietly as before, "It's not far now."

The slums enclosed us, and the ancient narrow houses leaning over on each other. The cats' eyes of the lamps seemed to float in the air, watching us.

Then we came to a row of shops, beyond the lamps and not a light anywhere in the shuttered windows above or to either side. He let go of me and went up a stair, opened a door, beckoned to me. I could just see that movement, the gesture of a ghost. I must go up, and so inside, and there whatever he would do to me he would do, and then he would pay me, and I could go. I followed as far as the doorway. And there I halted, staring in blank incomprehension. I could not think or reason. Only my body was afraid.

"Please step inside, Mademoiselle."

The distant lamplight described him after all. He carried a mountain on his shoulders, a hunchback. But his face was like an overgrown boy's, with an expression of unfathomable simplicity. I shrank from him; he seemed to have no complexity for which I could feel sympathy, against which any barrier could be erected.

"I'm sorry," I said. "I don't think I'm able to, after all."

"Oh," he said, "but you must. Look." And he held out towards me now the leaf of the note. "Just be a little kind," he said, "just a little kind, then you can have the money." And he put out his hand very lightly to touch my breast.

Somehow, I jumped back from him and at the same time I snatched the bill from his fingers.

A thief. A cheat. One more dog gnawing the vitals of another.

I turned and ran. And although his boy's face had not seemed to alter, of course he came after me. I heard his footsteps landing unevenly on the outside stair as I sped over the cobbles, clutching my box, the stolen bill. Even as I began my flight, I had thought: *You fool. He needs and must have the money. He'll never let you get away.*

It was so dark. Where had all the street-lamps gone to? The cobbles, slick with the breath of rain, turned the heels of my shoes, made for elegance not running.

And in my purse, clutched with box and bill, my book, Lucien running with me.

Rather sell hand or eye, you said, than the painting in your book. But you would not sell the only part of you which would fetch a price in Troy.

Never in all my life until tonight had I stolen anything, or taken anything which did not belong to me, while for so many among the poor stealing was a way of life, exactly and unalterably that.

Lucien had in the beginning also been poor.

Scribbling his frenzied diatribes against *l'injuste* in an attic room, the stove unlit, the only warmth the candle – but the candle is put out…

I could hear the plodding merciless footfalls ever behind me, not gaining but not dropping back. I should never escape.

Why had I done it? I had known at once, even before my fingers closed on the crisp paper, that I would fail.

Turning a corner in blackness, there was mud underfoot and I slipped, stumbled. The lacquer box and all the little it contained, the last fragments that had made up the external world for me, crashed on to the street. For a second I hesitated, half crouching to gather up what I had lost. But the relentless blundering of the hunchback came closer. I sprang up again and fled on, lightened now, holding only my purse, and the bill I no longer wanted, which seemed to weigh me down like a bar of lead.

I suppose it came quickly, the moment when I knew I could go no further. As a hunted thing will, then, I turned for a pitch-black hole, a burrow into which I could scramble. There was one. A kind of alley between two walls. Down this I scurried, my lungs choked by fire, blinded and mad.

So I became aware too late that the dark tunnel ended in a burst of light. I tried to clear my eyes, to see what I had rushed into, but light and blackness wheeled over my head, the very sky was falling on me with the thick sweetish smell of dried grass. Then I had run against a living wall, the body of a man, which seemed colossal, a great hard fat bolster of stuffing, and a hot breath of garlic, tobacco, humanity, which appalled me, but which somehow made me able to speak.

"Behind me," I cried, indicating, I thought, my pursuer. And I thrust the note up in the air like the flag of truce. "Give it him, monsieur. Give it him for me. For the love of God. I don't want it."

That was all I could manage. I let go of the bill, not knowing if I had been relieved of it, or if it had only fallen to the ground. Then I slid down the wall of flesh and lay on the cobbles, and I thought foolishly, *it's over. Now I can rest.*

I did not faint. I was conscious of what went on about me, though it seemed a vast way off.

Someone ran into the tunnel, though not as far as I had done, up to the light. The fat man walked over to him.

"Yours, I think, sir. Yes?"

"It is mine," I heard the cool voice of the hunchback say. He did not seem out of breath, or angry, even now.

"Then you won't be needing the young

woman for anything, will you?"

"No, monsieur. I'm sorry to have troubled her."

"A misunderstanding, I expect."

"Quite so."

Then one set of footsteps went calmly away. Another set came back. My saviour stood over me.

"Thank you," I muttered.

"What?" I felt his warmth as he bent near, but did not see him.

"*Beau merci*, monsieur." I would have said more, but I was too tired. At last I said, "Don't bother about me, monsieur. I'll get up m a moment, and be on my way. Just let me rest a little. A minute." Having begged him for a minute's ease lying on the rainy cobbles, I relaxed. There was nothing more to do.

But he said, "You can't rest there," and then he lifted me, stood me on my feet, and began to propel me forward. I did not protest. He was only going to see me off whatever premises I was on. Soon, there would be another stretch of pavement, or perhaps a doorway, where I could lie down again. I held my purse firmly, afraid I would let go. Otherwise my arms, my legs had no feeling. It was the fat man, not I, who kept my body upright.

Then we passed right through the dazzle of

light. I heard a clatter and something snorted. "Hush, children," the man called softly. There were horses there, and the musky-sweet grass odour was hay. Then the light was gone. There was a dark opening. We went into it. Something new, hard and inanimate, (a chair), held me.

"Madame!" The fat man stood bawling. "Madame!"

A pause then. During the pause, something so strange. Because of my state, I did not question it at all. Seated there, only partly conscious, my eyes shut, reality far off, I sensed the pale pearly blooming of another light, that of a lamp, somewhere above me. And in the depths to which I had descended, the night of misery and despair, the waking of that lamp seemed like a touch, gentle and familiar, like a kiss even, such as a mother gives to a child she loves. There was no rationale to any of this, but I felt it, and it steadied me, heart and mind, so that at last my sight cleared and I could see again.

The tall fat man who had saved me was talking to a person on the landing of some stairs, explaining something about my arrival and condition – now I could see once more, my hearing served me less acutely.

Naturally, I looked up the stairs, so mean

and dark, to the source of the lamp. My first impression was blurred. A slender young girl stood there, her head aureoled by fair, loosely-curling hair, her shoulders and breast crossed with a *fichu* of cream lace. There seemed nothing out of the ordinary. Rather, I felt again that peculiar, unsubstantiated feeling of safety, of refuge.

Then my perspective altered. What I was seeing was a gaunt old woman, like something from a funfair, dressed in the clothes of a museum dummy. And from the lamp-glow, the eyes glaring again into mine. Fearsome eyes, demanding something un-named, impossible, and terrible. Madame Two Swords. It was to her, her very doorstep, that I had run.

…at one time, it was the fashion to drown in the river…

…it seemed like this, as though I had stepped backwards…

FOUR

Then she gestured to me, jerking the lamp; I knew she meant me to go up. I had risen, when the man interpreted, "Madame means you to – ah, yes."

I started to climb the stairs, and at once she turned and went on ahead of me, back to the place she had emerged from.

I was trembling with weakness and clung to the rail. It seemed to me I must not lose sight of the lamp. The shadow of her figure, moving before me, appeared again that of a young and graceful woman.

We were climbing to the second floor, I understood that now. Here was the storey above the courtyard where the painted board had hung, the advertisement for her curious and supposedly unsavoury exhibits. Up to that we went, to the – what had the sly carter told me those eight years in my past? – the musical boxes made of skulls, the tarot cards, death-masks.

What had brought me here? Some confused memory in the swirling blindness of panic and night?

At the top of the stair there was a passage with a closed door on either side. The old woman, the young, *she* went on between, and I followed as if mesmerised. At the end of the passage came a turn to the left. As the lamp moved to one side it flung up a wing of light and caught a portrait hanging on the discoloured paper. The image was momentary, almost like an illusion of a man's face, dark hair, vanishing as the lamp withdrew into the angle of the wall. Nevertheless, though I did not know the picture, had never seen it reproduced, I knew its subject. It was Lucien de Ceppays.

I had stopped dead. I waited for the light to come back, to show me again. And sure enough, the light did come back. It ran straight up the wall to the pallid olive-complexioned face and the burning eyes. He looked very different in this second portrait, yet I had known him. He wore a green velvet coat, immaculate linen, fine gloves. He had ridden to prosperity on the Revolution's back, like so many others. He seemed to look at me. His eyes were like hers in their clarity, their intensity, the eyes of the old woman.

She spoke to me then, for the first time.

"Yes, it's a splendid painting, mademoiselle. And worth something." Her voice was like a wire, so rusted, yet so hard and absolute. "You know the young man it depicts?"

I could not speak. I nodded once.

"I possess others, other paintings, likenesses. You will find he looks differently in each. Sometimes, he would seem very ordinary, at others they said even ugly. But sometimes handsome, mademoiselle. When he addressed the crowds, mademoiselle, when he was full of that fire – then he was beautiful." She paused. "So they say. Even in the death cart. One of the women in the crowd shouted to him that he would make a pretty corpse. He said…"

"Though you paint an inch thick, lady, someday so will you." I had not meant to or known I would interrupt her.

She seemed startled, even shaken. when I supplied those words.

"What?" she said, "you know it all, then."

"No," I said. "No, Madame."

The light wavered. "No," she agreed. Then she took away the illumination again, and again somehow I found the strength to follow her. As I passed beneath his portrait, it was as if a soundless voice whispered something in my ear. The *frisson*, not of fear but of *discovery*, moved over my head and neck. What the discovery was I did not know. I knew nothing.

I barely looked at the room she led me into. I asked her permission to sit, and dropped into a chair, very old and worn but antique, and probably priceless. I let my head fall back, and felt powerless ever to move again.

After a long time, it seemed I was alone. The lamp, or one very like it, burned on a little table with a red velvet shawl draped over. Beyond the lamp's radius all was vague.

Presently someone came in. I expected the old woman, or her driver. (I had fitted the fat man with the glimpsed figure on the box of the carriage). But instead it was a servant girl, smartly dressed in a perfectly contemporary way. She drew up another small table to my chair and placed for me a bowl of steaming soup, bread, a goblet of wine.

"And I will bring coffee in ten minutes," she said to me, brightly, as if promising a treat to a child.

A treat indeed.

Oh, how good the simple food tasted. Every flavour in the soup stung my palate. The wine was smooth as honey, dry as wormwood, and so warming. The blood began to move in me again, and my heart to beat. She, or one of them, had known exactly what to supply after the weeks of semi-fast. I think if they had given me chicken or pastry it might have been like murder; I would have eaten it and died.

Before the coffee came, I fell asleep in that momentous chair. I had become aware of a fire burning in the room, of pictures and furnishings, but all unspecified. Perhaps this was a house of my enemies, or of lunatics. But so far they had not hurt me. They had taken me in without one question asked. Suddenly I was sheltered, cared for. What else did I need to know?

It was only that I sensed I had been summoned here. Drawn, inveigled – something of the sort. Perhaps witchcraft was real and I its victim. *What did she want from me?*

Or was it Lucien de Ceppays who had been the catalyst? Out in the unlit passage, the portrait hung like a great green jewel – where one only saw it on entering, or going forth.

You do not see pictures of him often, in the city. His name is defaced as that of a misguided idealist; his poetry is reduced to beauty, and his pamphlets to historical curios. The *Francais* rule France, even while the invisible strings of the puppet-masters lift them up and pull them down. It is safer to obscure, but not to hide altogether, the excesses of that former time, now two centuries are securely between us.

I woke at some unnamed hour, only for a moment, and noticed the rug wrapped around me. As they had not yet questioned me I did not, in my mind, yet question them.

There were many dreams but by that time I woke they were already far away, and in the morning only the taste of them lingered, faint and fading as the scent of flowers after rain.

In the morning too, I was restored enough to be very nervous. But nothing had gone wrong. Further luxuries fell on me like thrown ribbons. There were hot rolls and hot-house oranges and the strong coffee I had missed the night before. There was a bathroom with a marble bath that was filled with steaming water for me by Madame's sprightly maid. Toothpaste and brush, soap and sponge were set ready for me, and in the next room, on the *vanité*, a comb and hair-brush, even a bottle of cologne. When I came to dress again, my shabby clothes had been virtuously dusted and ironed, and there were fresh undergarments and stockings, not extravagant but of good quality. I had tried tentatively questioning the maid, but she was full of gossip, twittering like a happy bird. She never stopped talking, seeming to tell me more than my mind could hold, in fact telling me very little... I did hear that she had been sent out early to purchase items for my convenience. It was quite reasonable, if a cause of astonishment, to believe her. And yet, finding so many things to hand had heightened that sense I had of having been expected, therefore enticed, to come.

The room adjacent to the bathroom was mine, I was told. It had been shut up some time, but now the fire was lit and the windows thrown open. It was not a large room, the bed filling most of the space, an old-fashioned bed, of course, with carved posts. The *vanité* had lost its mirrors, but on the wall above there was a beautiful tarnished looking-glass set in silver-gilt, and underneath a silver candlebranch, filled with candles, and placed there quite casually. I somehow had the notion that before the influx of the current furniture, this had been a child's room.

Across the hallway was a closed door – Madame's chamber. Apart from these rooms, the rest of the floor was unused.

It seemed the maid was the coachman's daughter, and slept in his accommodation across the yard. Cooking was carried on at a baker's downstairs.

Almost involuntarily, I asked if the bookshop were still there. "Oh, no, mademoiselle," the maid said. "They sell wine there now." But I thought she looked at me oddly when I asked.

All the time I was on tenterhooks, waiting for the moment when I should be required to present myself once more to my benefactress, the mad, appalling old woman in her gown two centuries out of the mode. It was true, I felt an attraction as well. She, too, was concerned with Lucien. She possessed at least one rare and valuable picture of him. Even her way of dressing was an accolade to the female fashions of his day. I had begun to form a terrifying, electrifying notion that she was in line of descent from him. In this way, I seemed close to her; the alarming twist to my destiny became apt if not logical.

Finally, I could bear the suspense no longer.

I said to the maid, who had come back again to make up the ancient bed: "Am I to see Madame?"

"Whenever you wish, mademoiselle. Madame is a little poorly today, but her instruction was that you go across and knock at her door as soon as you're ready."

My heart turned over. I stood. I said, "Is she

very frail?"

"Why yes, mademoiselle. She's very old, you see. But hardy, too."

"How old?" I said. It seemed discourteous and harsh to ask.

The maid smiled, flapping the sheets that were pale yellow with age but fine, smelling of roses and cinnamon.

"Well, my father says nearly a hundred. That's a great age, isn't it?"

"Yes, a very great age."

"He's always been with her, man and boy, as he says. And his own father before that. They were in the country then. But that was long before I was born."

"And Madame's children?"

"Oh, there are no children. Or there may have been a child, but it died. Isn't it awful, mademoiselle, how many children die every year? I was reading about it in the paper. And the children on the *quais*, with all the rats – shocking, mademoiselle. My father says it will never get better, nothing will be done. But there I am, chattering on. Excuse me."

A moment more and I found I was in the narrow hall, my hand raised to knock at Madame's door. I was half afraid to do it, but the maid was watching me with her glossy gaze through the partly-open bedroom door-way. I had no option.

My hand fell on the panels. It was a wonder she heard the timid noise. Unless she had been waiting for it. At the sound of her voice, her voice like a wire, I started again unaccountably. Then I opened the door as she bade me, and went in.

I had expected to find her propped up in some enormous bed, the elder cousin of the one I had been allotted. But no. The bed was not large; a girl's bed, for one occupant alone, and modern, if not new. The other was the marriage bed, the bed of love and sex and comfort, now relegated to dust-sheets, or to sudden guests. It seemed indecent to think of her private reasons in this way, standing before her, but the idea was positive. In any case, she was not in the slender, maidenly bed of disappointment or widowhood, but seated in a chair by the bedroom fire, a rug over her knees and a pillow at her back, rather as I had been seated last night.

She sat and looked at me, and said not a word. Her thin skin seemed to hold the fire inside itself, luminous, like dulled porcelain.

"Madame," I said, "my gratitude…" and began to stammer with agitation, something that had not happened to me since my adolescence.

What stopped this jagged inconsequential flow was her face. It turned so white under its original faded whiteness I was afraid for her. Coherence returned to me. I asked, "What have I said?"

"Why do you stutter like that?" she said. Her look was pitiful. I felt it like a wound, aching somewhere inside me. What had I done to hurt her? Nothing. She was mad.

"I'm sorry," I said firmly. "I'm overcome. No one has been kind to me, as you have been kind, for some while." This, when out, sounded like pleading or fawning, and I felt myself flush, to complement her blanch of mysterious pain. "I have no means to repay you. But when…"

"Do I ask for repayment?" She was hard again. She glared at me almost with hatred.

"I did not mean to imply – but to take me in – your man will have told you about the…" I paused, to collect myself. I said, "I stole something. I was frantic and didn't know what I was doing, if that will serve as an excuse."

"Did I ask you either, mademoiselle, for explanations?"

Several things went through my mind. At a loss, I abruptly decided I must confront her. Now was the time when perhaps I would learn I must take flight again. But it was better to know too soon than too late.

"I presume," I said, "that you want something from me." She sat there. She watched me. Nothing else. "You remember you saw me as I left the cemetery. You do remember, Madame? Two days ago. It seemed to me then – I don't know. But it seems to me still that – I came here as a destitute, perhaps a criminal, and you don't ask explanations, as you say, or repayment. And so what *do* you ask, Madame? Please tell me. I may not be able to give it. And then your hospitality would be abused."

She went on sitting, not answering or moving, and it became intolerable. The fire crackled, a clock ticked somewhere, I felt the heavy thudding of my heart. She affected me in so strange a way, ominous, and yet – I could not tell what it was, the bittersweet anguish, as if she reminded me of some loss. My mother and I had never been very close. There was affection between us, the often easing companionship of habit. But though I had wept once or twice for the sadness of her life, her wretched death, they were the tears of the essential stranger.

And this one was not like my mother. This witch of the swords.

Finally, I saw her lips open, actually saw it in

a sort of slowed motion. Thank God, the endless silence was to be broken. But how she broke it.

"Lucien," she said, "Lucien de Ceppays. What is *he* to *you*?"

And now utter silence was my portion.

What was I to say? My *raison*, my hope? A stupid schoolgirl dream never outgrown? The only aspiration, the only glimpse of flame in my grey sluggish unimportant life? My talisman? Crucifix? My sanity? The love of my soul? Always, he had been my secret. I read of him in private. The little book, the portrait in its cameo, (shown to none), these were my candles. It was the business of no other. He was *mine*.

And yet. That other portrait hung in the dark of the gloomy passage, the coat, green for spring, the blazing eyes and elegant hands. She knew so much more of him than I. (He looks differently – sometimes very ordinary, at others ugly. Sometimes handsome – beautiful.) She even dressed for him. He, by some curious means, though hardly less so than mine, surely, was also hers.

In the end, I managed to say quite flatly and idly, "Why, Madame, most people know about him, who know anything of the city's history. Why should that seem odd to you?"

"Ah no, *ma chère*," she said, "it does not seem odd to me; it is you yourself who react so curiously to your own knowledge."

I shrugged.

She said, "You don't answer my question."

"And you, Madame, have answered none of mine."

She looked away from me, into her fire. I did not know what to do. I should of course leave at once, but that was not easy. I would need huge strength to do that. And I seemed to have no strength at all at this moment.

Just then the door was rapped and immediately opened. The contemporary maid came through beaming, as if all were well, were splendid. She carried a tray with extraordinary fare upon it, the food of those who can afford to eat consistently and nicely. I stared at the cold meats and the cheeses, the bread wrapped in its napkin, from which the smoke of heat still rose, the chocolate in the plumed pot.

Having set the tray down next to her employer, the girl reached to plump the pillow, twitch the rug. "More coal for the fire, Madame?" I saw these were the attentions not of a wise servant who valued her job, but of a child who had grown up in proximity and love.

"No, don't trouble, Janette." The old woman smiled at the smiling girl. That smile, that smile. The ruined face, hanging as it seemed by a thread of life, and the ghosts behind it. One felt that to rip away the outer covering, that tissue of lizard's skin, would be to find again beneath the firm white flower of youth and loveliness. But she said, taking the young girl's hand an instant, sighing, "How tired I am today, Janette."

"Shall I fetch the cordial, Madame?"

"No. It's all very well. But this tiredness – I find it not unpleasant."

The maid of the *Frenish* name, *Janette*, frowned. To her, tiredness could not be pleasant. Existence was work and bustle, and then maybe to dance five or six hours under rainbow lamps, to sleep as short a space as negotiable, then to start up and begin again.

When the maid was gone, we drank chocolate, but my stomach, so long denied, rebelled against this regularity of feasting. Besides, everything disturbed me. The sight of the old woman's hand trembling from frailty on the fragile cup, as yesterday my own had done from hunger, tore at my heart.

I did not understand my sensations of pity. They were greater than compassion. I longed to go to her and put my arm about her, to console her, promise her better things. It was absurd.

"It was the drive tired me," she said

eventually. "That long drive in the Bois, and then along the road from the cenotaph, past the cemetery gate. Something made me do it. I don't like to drive out anymore, and the cars worry the horses. Yes, I saw you. You have heard things about me, from the days when I read hands, or when my exhibition, surely the grimmest in Troy, was open to the public. Very few visited the exhibits. In the end, I could not bear them myself. The rooms were closed, the objects, many of them... dispersed. It was a museum of the Revolution, mademoiselle. Anger must be used; fear, also. Should you like to see the exhibition? I can open it for you. There are five representations of Monsieur de Ceppays, who intrigues you so much. The sixth hangs in the passage. There was a seventh. But that..." she gazed at me, "that seventh small picture was sold. For a pittance. The fool that bought it did not know the worth... But then again, it wasn't done for money, mademoiselle. You understand? Some things become too precious, or too harmful. They should be given away."

I was cold. Even my hands which held the hot cup seemed made of ice. All at once I knew. The madwoman. It was she who had brought to the bookshop, across this very yard, the book bound in blue cloth with the water-colour between its covers. She. So many years ago. And now she had reconsidered, and learned, by some inconceivable means, that I possessed it. And she meant to take it back.

And though I had bought the picture, still I had no right to it beside her rights, which were incalculable.

"You eat nothing," she said. "Janette will be *frustré* after all her effort. Come, then. Come, and I'll show you my museum."

And she rose, casting off the rug, and all apparent infirmity with it.

I had not left my purse in my room but brought it here with me, the painting safe inside. I had felt threatened long before I grasped the nature of the threat. How clever I had been in that.

…what I saw in the mirror was Lucien…

FIVE

I had seen only oil-lamps, candles, and had not thought any of the floor equipped for gas. But my hostess thrust open the door and gaslight there was, already lit for us, presumably by Janette, throughout the 'museum'. The order must have been given long before Madame received me in her bedroom. She had always intended to bring me here.

I did not want to go into the museum of the Two Swords. The carter's warnings? No. My reasons were less sensible and more overwhelming. Nameless, formless reasons. Yet I did not refuse. How could I? To humour Madame would be the best course, the only course.

The entrance lay through that left-hand door at the head of the passage, one of the pair I had passed between last night. The architectural construction of the museum was rather eccentric, and no doubt effective for being so. It occurred to me presently that it followed the line of the building around, descending or going up stairs as it literally climbed over or under or behind the other occupied areas: Madame's own lodging, the baker's below, and so on. Eventually it returned itself to the entry passage – by the second door of the pair. No doubt, Madame had arranged the foibles of partitioning and staircases, utilising where able the vagaries of storerooms and cupboards. There were no windows. Where they had existed, brick and plaster had smothered the evidence. Only pale flickering gaslight lit the way; only the shadows of gaslight underlined it.

One did not get directly into the first room. There was a curtain there, just inside the entrance. Was it here the entry fee had been paid? Madame moved to the curtain, but did not hold it aside or go on. It was to me she motioned. I must enter first.

Reluctantly, my purse clutched in one frozen hand, I parted the dusty drape and passed through.

I had been braced for a shock of some kind. Not knowing what it would be had made expectation all the worse. But the rectangular space was not really startling. Except that, on the wall facing you as you entered, there hung the three-colour banner of the Revolution, an emblem no longer publicly seen in this form. Everywhere else, up on the walls, lying on tables down the room, were the dark mementoes of that explosive season. Muskets, butchers' knives, a piece of melted ordnance dragged from La Tour after it fell, a slab of wall from the same edifice, with the pathetic, often obscene scribblings on it of its pessimistic captives. Between all this hung etchings of the city as it had been two hundred years ago, on the brink of turmoil, or caught in the actual tumult of revolt. And by these, the documents of upheaval and alteration. If originals, they were beyond evaluation, and originals they seemed to be. A proposed constitution on brown parchment hung beside a hand-written bill of human rights with marks at two corners of the paper where the nails had been hammered and later on ripped out.

I wandered in the room, not touching anything, though all was laid out bare as if specifically authorising contact, actual handling. A sourceless, electric tingling seemed to move in the air, as if everything remained alive, the rage, the shouts of the starving mob, the exhilaration of beginnings. Intuitively, I hurried towards the first of the twisting wooden stairs, going down. I felt a need to progress swiftly. Because of my obsession with Lucien de Ceppays I had always, formerly, been very interested by things of this era. But here I seemed able to keep no distance, was about to be swallowed up by the raw echoes of emotion still ringing so loud. In this windowless world, despite the gas-light, La Tour might only have fallen a week ago, and these souvenirs been lugged here yesterday. At any moment, the crowd might come rushing up through the house to take them back for another assault...

Just by the wooden stair I came across one of the carter's tales come true. A sword hung black-green on the plaster. It was one of the swords of execution which had sipped, so its label claimed, the blood of three princesses, twenty lords, and one marshal of Troy. Underneath on a ledge lay a skull, polished and lacquered, with an inscription in seed-pearls which said: *Je suis le Prince de Polignac. Etendez-vous!*

"Raise the upper part from the jaw and this contrivance plays a popular Revolutionary song."

I shivered as the old woman spoke. I had

almost forgotten her, and yet she seemed omnipresent as the electric air.

"For God's sake no, Madame."

"Yes, it's a horrid thing. But the museum shows what aspects it is able. And there were toys made later, tiny *guyotines*, with tiny blades which could almost take off a finger. They were very common. But I keep none here. Go on. Down the stair. There is more to see."

I glanced at her. The gas-glare, or what she did, made her look ill. I could think of nothing to say, but as if I might she made a gesture of lightly pushing me, goading me on.

The stair was dim and I went carefully. I had begun to feel a sort of generalised inertia and sick sensitivity, as if at the onset of fever.

At the stair's foot, looking up, I stopped with an intake of breath. The second room was full of people. "Ah," she said behind me, and then a little laugh, like a girl's.

No, they were not real, the figures, though they were life-size and tinted and dressed to the life. Like huge dolls they poised, caught in the activity they were intent both to facilitate and to show off. It was a vast printing press, black, scrolled with the paws and masks of lions. Rolls of paper lay about, curling and uncurling. A man in shirt-sleeves and leather apron attended to the weights. I walked between the elegant statues in their nankeen coats, cravats like butterflies or bandages, (curious, that fashion at such a time, when heads rested so loosely on the neck), their smooth culottes and white stockings. There was no dust on the press, or on the tableau. They were cared for still, it seemed.

The pamphlets piled up from the press, several of which a man in blue held out to me, were the *Debate Between the Gallows and the Aristocrat*. I turned as if someone had called my name, and there stood Lucien de Ceppays.

He was taller than I am, a tall slim elegant male doll among dolls. He had been dressed in the green coat of the portrait, with a pale sky-blue waistcoat, buff breeches, doe-skin gloves. The fashionably tilted hat had the green leaves pinned to it of the *Marche Printemps*. The dark hair curled on his shoulders and sprang about the snowy cravat. Under the long brows, the black eyes looked down into mine.

The old woman said nothing. I stared, speechless and unthinking and motionless, with pandemonium inside me.

As she had said, always he looked different. And yet, the same. Here, he was solemn and beautiful as an angel sent among the blood and slime of anarchy, to ennoble the desperation of men. But through the witty prose and the blaze of his poetry, he had dispatched the hosts of victims on and on towards the scaffold that, eventually, would also accommodate him. At the end, he had known it. Who live by swords die by them.

Suddenly I could not bear it, its reality, the truth and the lie, personified in this life-size figure.

I ran across the room of waxworks. I ran up another twisting, squinnying stair. There was next a gallery with countless portraits, busts, folios – so many they overlapped each other like the scales of fish. Pictures of Lucien doubtless hung here, but I could not halt to find them. I dashed about the circuit, eager only to escape. It was too much, too much. I could not reason. I seemed split in two.

Down again. A room of garments, books, a cannon-ball, manifestos, seals and keys. I had left Madame, the witch, far behind. My procedure was sharp before me. I should eventually reach the passage again and so the stairway to the yard outside. I would abscond. I would not stay for any more, not for food, for shelter, not to explain or ask pardon. She preyed on me. This place. Or I – myself. What it was I did not know.

More twisting stairs. Up again. I panted from dread, not haste. There was a kind of vestibule. I pushed past another curtain. And cried out.

And ceased to run.

It seemed like this: As though I had stepped backwards – no, as if I had been flung back – through time. And yet, so much was missing, the noise, the very stink of those masses who pressed all about me. And the open air, the spring sky beginning to darken, the chocolaty smell of burning as the first torches were lit. And the guardsmen drummers, whose drumsticks did not move. Missing, the rattle and jar of the tumbril as it juddered over the cobblestones, and the rain of flowers and eggs, and the reek of old blood.

Here it was already night, the dramatist's licence. Just one distant rift of red, against which, in blackest silhouette, the *guyotine* stood upright on its hill. And the pack of spectators, into whose midst I had run, as if to be one of them, were chill and smooth, odourless, unbreathing, against me. To my left, a woman waved a static handkerchief stretched on a wire, which made it seem to float. A man held up a child to see, and the child craned, its sallow face smudged with a dirt that was only picturesque. Although the predatory excitement, that had been faithfully and cunningly represented, the vulpine grins of broken teeth, the fear which had turned, once more, to vengeance. This second tableau was as excellent, perhaps better than the other.

Between the crowd and the distant *guyotine*, the death cart was passing, drawn by plodding horses whose glass eyes winked sadly. Ribbons on wires fluttered in an unending moment of time.

The men in the cart were Lucien and those who had died in his company that evening. Two held each other. One was shouting, his arms raised and black hair blown back. The finery was all gone. Stripped to their shirts, the linen stained and torn, bare-headed. These glass eyes, in the oddly angled lighting, seemed full of madness or tears. The man shouting was Lucien. I had never read that he had done so. His face was twisted with fury and terror and dismay and hate. He was ugly. The stage at which he had promised flirtatious Shakespearian death to the young woman with her taunts of 'pretty corpse' was obviously done. He had fought for them and in the end they had pulled him down like the wolves. He had sung to them, wooed them, been loved by them and loving. He would have killed them now.

"He always feared her, *la Canaille*," she said, Madame, who had caught me up after all, since I had been rooted here some while. "He said, 'Times change, men change, the rabble – never.

77

The rabble is an animal, a corporate body made up of many atoms of which each of us, however delicate or refined of soul, is capable of becoming part. It is a mindless beast, needing and wanting only hot blood to feed on and the warmth of itself for a home. Few men have never felt the lure of it, or the joy of it, being in, if only for a second. To many it is like strong drink.' That is what he said. And what he knew. How else could he move them as he did? In the beginning, he feared a crowd so much he couldn't speak, couldn't make himself heard. His voice would stick in his throat like a piece of poisoned apple. So it must all be said in print. The pamphlets, the poems, these roared what he could not. But in the end, in the end the flood-tide swept over him as well. That young man whose only voice had been a pen, that stammering boy, shouting like a bell. An orator. The touchstone. Spring is on the march! And they marched, mademoiselle. Through the city, through the rubble of La Tour, over the severed heads and through the forests of hanged men. They marched against *Les Anglais* and were beaten back. They turned and ran. They scattered like mad dogs, savaging whatever lay in the path. Lucien – lay in the path. They had made him one of their princes, the princes of the *bourgeoisie*. They would have to drag him to the scaffold. What else are saviours and princes for? Calvary, always Calvary."

The lighting was bizarre. I could not see her, only a shadow of a young girl dressed for the tableau, who spoke with the voice of a hag.

There seemed no point now in head-long flight. This room was cast from black despair, one could not be immune to it. I turned slowly. In an alcove, a gas-lamp burned. Fiendishly lit, the death-masks of the men in the cart looked down with forever-blinded open eyes.

"These things," she said, and I heard her moving, her antique dress rustling, through the waxwork crowd. "Some I have collected, some I have had made. An artist with some talent and no soul, he took the impressions for the masks when the heads lay like warm fruit still in the basket."

They were all famous men. But I had found Lucien's mask. The eyes were wide, but the lips only slightly parted as if about to ask a question.

"And the last words he spoke," she said. "Do you know what they were? He was calm at the end. I will tell you; several overheard. He said, 'Camélie, Camélie, Camélie, Camélie, Camélie.' Over and over. Only that. *Camélie, Camélie*.... Have you heard of her, mademoiselle?"

"His – mistress." I did not know why I

answered.

And she responded harshly. "His *wife*. You're ill-informed after all. He married her a few days before his arrest. He loved her. He would say, 'Let me be quiet with you, Camélie.' He would say, 'The only peace I know in the world is with you'."

"And the child?" I said.

"It died," she said. "It wasn't loved enough. Once he was dead, there seemed no love left, to take or to give."

I would not glance at her. I stared on at the blank stony egg of Lucien's mask.

"To wish to die so much," she said. How old, how old she sounded, insubstantial, like powder falling from ancient lace. "Ah, how she wanted to die, did Camélie de Ceppays. She wrote to the tribunal, the puppets who had accused and condemned her husband. *Kill me too*. She insulted them, those things passing for men. On the streets, in the halls of Injustice. Even at the burial she cried out the forbidden cry of the old order which they must suppress. Prison then. More than once she saw the insides of the dungeons of Troy, the dungeons that had held her love the last night of his life. But her life they would not take. *Madame*, one of those great administrators said to her, *you must think me mad. We do not need one more beautiful young martyr. You're too pretty to die so publicly. You would get us a bad name, with your sweetness, and your beautiful eyes.* Because I was beautiful then, mademoiselle. And for a long time after. A long, long time. God has been very cruel to me," she said. "He's let me grow old alone. But the only thing I wanted, that he's refused. To be with Lucien, to be with him wherever he is, in air, in fire, in everlasting nothingness. To die. Oh, how I've yearned for death. But I cannot die, you see. The child, yes. Hope, oh, *yes*. And beauty and all things. Even hatred and anger died at last, and the museum of hatred and anger was put away. But the grief never dies. Grief is my flesh, my heart, my very spirit. And so I am immortal. Like my grief."

I had known, almost from the instant that she mentioned Camélie's name, that this confession would be the outcome.

Sickened and weighed down, I had no energy to resist. *I believed her.* She was also utterly convincing. She told me with a sort of helpless ennui. Yet her pride in the marriage, her voice when she used his name – they were convincing, too. I would in some way have recognised her as sincere, perhaps only with the sincerity of madness, if we had been anywhere save where we were. Here, recognition was inevitable. The toy theatre of death was at my back. The masks in a line before me. *Madame Deux Epées* at my side.

Deux Epées -- Two Swords -- a pun. All the time I had entertained the name as it was written, in English, I had not heard how the phonetic values were so similar as to be one: *Deux Epées*; de Ceppays. Madame de Ceppays. The wife of Lucien. Two hundred years of age. Prevented ironically, by the trauma of her wish for death, from dying. Yes, then, she had some claim on him.

But I said, "Madame, do you expect me to believe such nonsense?"

"I'm aware you do believe it," she replied.

"And is that why you brought me to your madhouse last night?"

"Brought you? How would I do that?"

"I – how am I to know? You're the sorceress, Madame. You have had two hundred years to learn such tricks. Or perhaps the hunchback was your agent."

I did look at her then. Lucien's mask was so cold on my eyes. Her withered lunacy seemed warmer.

But again the curious light, the obscurity – again her face was a girl's, pure, pale, milk-glass, and the eyes made gentle by wounding. And she was afraid. She had summoned me by artifice or witchcraft. But she was as astounded by my advent, as frightened even, as I.

And then she shut her eyes and put her hand on the wall most pitifully. This room – to her, even if it were only some delusion, how much courage she had needed to have it made, a monument, a warning. And how much courage to enter it.

Before I could hesitate, I went to her, steadying and supporting her.

"The door is over there, Madame." She was light as a slender stick. We went towards the door I had only this moment discerned. "Not far now, Madame." I held her. Some scent came from her hair. I wanted to call her "Camélie." Her sorrow, true or false, had finally broken my heart.

We came out, as I had judged, in the passage above the stairs. I shouted for Janette. To my relief she came springing from the turn of the passage. Probably she had been waiting for all this excitement to prove too much.

We went, the three of us, slowly under Lucien's portrait. In the gloomy passage, without lamps, it was almost invisible.

SIX

As I was sitting on the great marriage bed an hour later, Janette came to the door.

"My father found this in the *Rue Jacobin*, mademoiselle, and thinks it may be yours. He never comes up into the apartments; Madame hasn't let any man up here for years. It's quaint, I say, and what if we should need the doctor, but there, I'm chattering on."

I watched her bring the box with the dragons painted on it across to the bed, and set it by me. It was certainly mine, the one that had cascaded from my arms in my flight from the hunchbacked man, (or from frying pan to fire). Not pilfered either, it would seem. Even the hair-brush had not run off, or the paper books, though spotted with dried rain.

"Thank you. Please thank your father." I did

not ask how he guessed the fugitive owned such a box spilled on the street. It was fairly obvious, no doubt.

I touched the assemblage, but no reassurance came from these well-known objects.

"How is Madame?"

"Very tired. Exhausted. As so." And she made the gesture of something collapsing without bones.

"Yes." I ran my finger along the serrated edges of the cracked shell mirror. "Janette, is her name truly Camélie de Ceppays?"

"Why, yes, mademoiselle. A distinguished family. From the country."

The immortal would learn how to conceal itself. How and where to hide, when to return. To dwell with a certain luxury in a poor alley, or retreat to some pastoral backwater. And discover, too, whom it could trust to serve it, and to tell lies or remain ignorant for its sake.

I changed my route. I said to the bright modern maid, "Did Madame expect me yesterday?"

"Expect you? *No*, mademoiselle. You were a nice old surprise for all of us."

"Then why take me in?"

"Madame's orders, mademoiselle. And you such a poor pale worn-out young lady…"

"So Madame makes a point of taking in

anyone who knocks at her door."

Janette said simply, "No one else has knocked, as Madame puts it, but herself."

Not meaning to, my hand strayed back to cover my purse and so the book inside it. Here I had sat all this while, guarding my crust like a fearful dog. Nor had I been able to leave. The mood of the museum clung to me yet, apathy and depression.

"On the other hand," said Janette, "since she drove out the other day, Madame's been that nervous. Is that a bird in the chimney? Is that someone calling? Are the horses fretful – go and ask Jean to see to them – my father, mademoiselle. And last might she paced about, up and down. Such an old lady, but a will like a diamond, it could scratch glass. It's the will has kept her so spry, my father says..." She broke off. I sensed that rather than render me information she had been using the rendition to see how I would react.

I said, "It's very strange, very strange," and pressed my fingers to my forehead, because I was unsure what to do.

Janette apologised, asked me if my head ached and went to fetch a chemist's preparation that I suspect had laudanum in it.

Meanwhile I listlessly sorted through my box. I had inadvertently lost my own life, but here it was again. Tonight, I must embark on it once more.

I should, of course, repay Madame for her generosity, though she seemed nearly to have killed my spirit on the road. Well, I could leave her the one thing she would value, could I not? The picture of Lucien she herself had painted, or she herself had imagined she painted, by the light of a guttering candle two hundred years ago. After all, I had been taught a lesson. My amulet had proved at last it too was a source of agony. And anyway, he was no longer mine.

But then, still I did not leave. Janette came to and fro, up and down, and the door to the other bedchamber opened and closed.

At length, I went to the drawing room where the fire was alight. Unshuttered, these windows looked out across the slate-blue roofs of the *Vieux Quartier* as far as that russet church with the great bell whose name I have forgotten, and beyond that to the clouded trees of the *Pré*. Dusk was beginning. The sun had already set, but the last birds flickered through the last light, settling back into the eaves and interstices reluctantly and fussily, as if too playful to want sleep.

It was peculiar, rather, to find the city still existed beyond this place, existed that is in the century in which I had left it. But I could hear the cars humming like monstrous bees on distant boulevards, and see a shop-sign written both in *Frenish* and in neon. Electricity is a perquisite of modern Troy, though few afford it.

Janette came in to me, inquiring about dinner, but my appetite was gone. I asked her again how was Madame Ceppays?

"Well, I've never seen her like this, mademoiselle, and that is the truth. I've been thinking of going across to find out what my father suggests now, since we both – that is, she's often tired, you understand. But this..."

I looked to see if Janette blamed me, but she did not seem to. Her cheerfulness had evaporated, however. I thought, my dear young woman, don't you know your employer is immortal? Don't your young glands scent it?

I believe Janette did indeed consult Jean the coachman. Later there was a vague altercation. Madame, it seemed, would have no one summoned. Of course not. A physician would be a fatuous recourse.

Sitting by the fire in the room of antique, priceless chairs, my purse on my lap, I did nothing. What was there to do but go, and I would not go. It would be imprudent to go, until things were a little quieter. And then, until

I knew how ill, or well she was... I had been implicated in something, if only by myself.

Finally, Janette brought wine, and some fish in a beautiful sauce, which I could not eat. Foolishness. Who could tell when I would be pampered this way again?

Finally too, it was late, close to midnight, and I went to the room I had been given, with the idea of taking some sleep, then stealing away, whatever my feelings, shortly before dawn. Such a plan certainly made me uneasy, almost unhappy. But all others were idiotic and would not serve, either myself, or – or her.

I lay down on the great bed, fully-clothed of course. I had not slept in it before, but in the chair in the other room. There was a kind of disorientation as I lay back. A sense of some sort of movement not quite apparent, as if the ground had shaken very slightly in a tremor. That was all.

I thought I was too tense to do more than doze, and that suited my purpose. I closed my eyes. And it began.

Monsieur Sandarac had shown me out on to the pavement by the Café Silver. He pointed away along the street. "Go up there, up there, that's the place for you."

Docile with fear and disgust I turned to obey

him. Something attracted my attention. The gutters were running with wine, or it might have been diluted blood. I looked up, and the priest who had buried my mother stood before me in his drab *soutane*, his hand outstretched for money. "But I paid you, *curé*."

"Not enough," he said. He held out his hand, held it out for ever. I had no money.

"There is a limit to what the poor can pay you," I said. My voice trembled. I thrust his hand aside and went on, and he let me.

A crowd of waiters stood outside a restaurant, idly swiping at broken glass with brooms, laughing. They laughed louder and pointed at me. I began to run.

But women came rushing from a gap in the wall, terrible women with mottled skin and sunken myopic eyes, and they seized me and rushed me away with them.

The sound of shouting was in my ears. It seemed I had been hearing it some time, had forgotten it, but now it came more violently and I remembered.

The cart jolted and bumped. They drove it slowly, for this was a carnival, and everyone should be permitted a good view. But we were across the bridge now *le Pont Trois Filles*. The cobbles went upward, and already there was, over the stink of the crowd, our own sweat and terror, the filthy smell of some great *abattoire*. But the journey had been tiresome. One wanted it to end.

"The foul reek of this place," someone said. "It will breed a plague, and I wish them much joy of it."

And someone else, "You've stopped yelling, Lucien? Splendid. I thought you'd deafen me. You suppose that wouldn't matter under the circumstances, gentlemen? Wrong. I mean to die, the perfect sacrifice, in full possession of everything."

A hand fell lightly on my shoulder.

"Look, there it is. The thin tall door marked Exit."

We looked and saw the instrument of oblivion standing up blackly on the evening sky of spring.

Before the first stars became visible, our eyes would no longer be capable of seeing them. And the throat, hoarse and burning, would be unable to produce another sound.

There was so much to be said, and they would not listen. *You see the death carts go by and you applaud, you mindless rabble, but it is your own selves, your own death you rejoice at. What are we – but you? What is our butchery but your own? Do you think we will be the last, or our destruction the destruction of your ills? No. This is their beginning.*

Useless, useless. They shout back, they scream and dance, jibing, throwing muck, in an ecstasy of unreason. Or some of them are dumb, staring at us as if at creatures in a menagerie.

And so much to do. So much. Never to be completed. And oppression riding now the crest of each great wave as it crashes scarlet from that falling blade. And at each stroke, the ground *shakes*.

Sweat in the hair, this sweat not like any sweat ever felt before, as if the body changes, knowing how soon, how totally it will be changed. And the texture of the hair, altered by it, unfamiliar. But down now, down on the shaking earth and the hands are bound. Oh yes, the hands are surely bound, the eyes put out, ears deafened, voices silenced forever.

A friend nudges me. Over there the monstrous artist is sketching us, the wretched sheep who await their slaughterer. The artist is due to take impressions of our dead faces once they are in the basket.

And tomorrow...?

The drums start, the blind-faced *soldats Anglais*. One of our number moves away, is herded up the ladder. He stumbles. Even his feet do not want to take him there. But to stumble is not enough. My God, he is a living man and now – and now the stroke comes down. And the crowd roar, and clap. And he...

But there were plenty before us. Plenty we sent over the *Pont Trois Filles*, up the hill under the edge of falling steel. Applauding the death of tyranny. Not seeing that death was ours.

And the other side of that blade, are they standing? Is there judgement? God and his angels, the long wait in the grave and then maybe to be cast down into the pit. But there is nothing the other side. All men know this secretly. The blank void of sleep instructs them. There is nothing.

What then to carry through this agony of fear and despair, as we shuffle closer and closer to unending night, what last candle, last image of light, for the blade to burn, for one last split second of pain and horror, into the dying consciousness? In the end, only one thing is worth having. Only one. That sweet lovely face against summer leaves, the kind hands, the kiss like cool water to thirst. Brave, beautiful, unreproachful Camélie. Calling after me down the stair, laughing. There in the heart of night. Sleep's anchor. Camélie. Camélie. ("What are you saying, Lucien?" "Let him alone.") Lovely, loving, loved. Lovely, loving...

And my feet are on the ladder now. (Camélie.) And the wood and metal are around

my neck and I must keep that thought of her,
God in pity let me keep it, until I hear the rasp
of the blade – God, God – only of her. Only of…

I was catapulted forward, so it seemed. As if
the engine of death had spat me out. Intact. For
I was whole. I raised my hands to my head – *an
escape*. The crowd, unable after all to endure the
lie, had torn the *guyotine* apart with its bare
hands, and in a laughing-crying hysteria we…

But I was alone, in darkness, sitting up on
the connubial bed of Camélie and Lucien, a
young woman in rumpled cheap clothing of
contemporary fashion, holding her head, her
throat, startled by life, by everything that
perhaps only an hour ago had been mundane.

Oh God, I said aloud, several times, each
repetition a ritual, calming me. Like Lucien, an
atheist, yet as he had done in my dream, I
called on the name of That in which I did not
believe. And eventually the repetition did calm
me enough that I got up from the bed and
fumbled my way through blackness to the
vanité, where the candles stood in their silver
sconces, and matches lay ready to hand.

I was not thinking, then; it was enough that I
had thrown off the tiger of the dream. Yet my
senses were acute. I found the match-box at
once, struck light unerringly and, half-blinded

by it, set it to each of the three candles. Then, as my sight was washed of the darkness, I raised my head, away from the candleshine and the objects on the *vanité*, and so looked into the tarnished ancient mirror in the silver-gilt frame.

In their manner, all mirrors are the slaves of truth. We are accustomed to their cruel lenses, which can sometimes flatter but never positively betray. We are used to seeing in a mirror what we have always seen there: Ourselves.

What I saw in the mirror was Lucien de Ceppays. He looked out at me, not blurred or wavering or translucent, not distorted in any way. He was there. I thought, if without words, this then is still the dream. But my eyes were clear. They met his eyes, across the two centuries between us. He was very like the cameo, and yet, unlike. It was as if I had misremembered him a little, as with old acquaintance sometimes one does, but now I beheld him I saw where I had been wrong. Here he was, the one I knew so very well. The details were exact. The sombre curling hair, the swarthy skin, the shirt open at the throat. There could be no mistake.

Perhaps I would not have moved, but some random air – maybe my own quickened breathing – disturbed the candle flames so they dipped and curtseyed. And in the looking-glass the candlelight which limned him too, also dipped, curtseyed, straightened – as if it were the same.

Instinctively then I put my hand to the front of my dress, felt there the high round collar and the velure buttons against my fingers' ends. But he too had placed his hand on his collar, the loose open collar of the shirt, and rested it there as I did mine.

Ah now, I thought, now this…

Ah now, he seemed to think, I glimpsed it in the black embers of his eyes, now this – is some joke.

And I caught in my breath, and so did he. And again the candles fluttered over my face and over his face, which was now the reflection of mine.

So I put out both my hands, and I saw them, my side of the mirror, the hands of a woman, white-skinned, chapped somewhat still from winter cold, with the tiny scar there I had had since childhood, and the small white fleck on the nail of the left index finger – and they met his outstretched hands, larger, darker, the long thin fingers with all the various idiosyncratic marks of their own – and there the writer's branding, the callous on the second finger where the pen would rest, where all my fingers were quite smooth.

I thought I must feel flesh in that moment. But there was only glass.

And so I knew.

My hands dropped from the reflection. I shut my eyes, and two hundred years breathed out from the mirror and were gone. When I looked again, I saw my mother's daughter in the candlelight, the nervous innocent feminine person I had been for twenty-two years.

I walked away from the *vanité* back to the bed, and sat there. I had some right to sit there, it seemed. I have never really believed in ghosts. I did not now believe in them. I knew what I had seen, what the mirror – which knew – or which I myself, who also knew, had made me the witness of.

In a life, one forgets so much, so soon. At twenty, how much of childhood remains, truly remains, intact? Incidents, yes, naturally, pictures, emotions, ambiences, flavours, but even these, no doubt, their edges softened by time, by all the fresh pictures, emotions, ambiences, flavours, which enter day by day. It is no accident the *vignette* is represented with its periphery melted into mist. So with the *vignettes* that are the episodes of life. Until at length the mist draws in, covering the whole of the image with its smoky veil. And if one life may be so forgotten, shall we not forget the land which lies behind the parting swords of death and birth, the life that was lived, and died, before this?

Although, not utterly forgotten, even then. I opened my purse and took out of it the little book, which Camélie had sold in her confusion and distress of soul, which I had bought in mine.

In the diluted candlelight, I held it. I glanced at the words of passion, authority and power. Suddenly tears blinded me. *I* had written them. *I*.

So long ago, far off, so much mislaid, the terror and the anger blotting out almost everything. Left incomplete, the smashed life, snapped in two pieces over the step of the *guyotine*.

Yet, like Camélie's grief, his anguish had not died. No, here it was. His anguish, his work, every hard lesson he had learned. And these, too, belonged to me.

I took the water-colour in my hands. I looked at myself as I had been. I looked a long, long silent time.

Camélie's painting of love. How could one ever think any but a lover had painted it? She had known him so surely. And love binds. Yes, he had been hers. For all this awesome nightmare of immortality she had endured, hers, hers. Still hers. That part of him retained in me was bound – to her yet. Camélie, lovely, loving, loved... That young girl on the summer day, putting her hand in his, laughing over the stair at him as he ran down towards the street. Yes, he was hers.

But also mine. Lucien was mine. He would be mine for ever.

I heard her crying then, the witch with her two eyes of swords, her desperate starving eyes, the endless youth of undying grief. She wept just as the infant does, as if there is nothing else but weeping. As if the hurt will never stop.

I went out quietly and across the narrow hall, and opened her door without knocking.

The room was full of the low red shadows of a settling, drowsing fire. I observed it all with a slight surprise, for I think I had been here long before, when the great bed had lain in place of the little one, and the child had slept with his nurse in the other room. The whole house had been very different, then, I imagine. Perhaps I would find some book that gave an account of it, and read, to remind myself, or to tantalise myself in failing to be reminded.

So much was unsure, and yet I had not a single doubt of any kind. I was like a blind woman given sight. I knew nothing, and yet I knew that these curiosities had always been here, and now I might regard them. No matter that I had fancied all objects otherwise, *this* was how they were.

In the slim heartless bed, she lay on her side, curled against banked pillows. She was crying in her sleep. As I went nearer, the firelight picked out a glass bowl on a table. It was full of pins and beads and silly little things; dusty, as though she had not touched them for a long while yet had not wanted them disturbed. I had not noticed the bowl before. Some trick of shadow or my perception had hidden it from me. Around the rim there twined a pattern of crocuses worked in yellow glass. Just such a bowl had formed the shade of that prized lamp of mine, stolen by the landlady. Perhaps it had once belonged with its fellow, here. A pair, each with something in it, apples, or short-stemmed flowers, or something of the child's, (miniature soldiers of coloured wood). The child which had shouted "Papa!" in a high disarming voice, but which had died.

I looked at her only a moment. Then I sat, and lifting her very gently I took her in my arms. As I rocked her, her tears stopped at last. She lay against me, lighter it seemed than any other substance I had ever held. Only a hair bound her to life, but it was a hair of steel.

The fire turned the colour of cherries, and then of damsons, and gradually went out.

But time was in abeyance. It lay waiting under the windows, imprisoned by night. The first light of dawn might cause it to move again, conceivably.

I had never felt such tenderness for my mother, who, in my way, I had loved. Such tenderness as this had its roots in other things. I did not recollect them. I might put them together only as a clever detective solves some crime, from a jigsaw of clues. And yet I knew that once she had been my refuge, as now, by some freak of circumstance and strangeness, I could be hers.

When the dawn did come, grey as the non-existent ghosts, along the sills, Camélie de Ceppays stirred in my arms.

"The book," she said. "The painting is still in the book?"

"Yes, my dear, I have it. I'm putting it under your hand."

We had spoken, both of us, not in the bastard *Frenish*, or the common patois of Troy, but in French, unmixed. She had known this language from her birth. I knew just enough.

She touched my book, running her fingers softly, in a caress, over the worn binding, the yellowed pages. Together, we looked down at the cameoed face of Lucien.

"I'd almost forgotten," she said. "One can forget so much in a few long years."

Poor little book, cracked and stained from being carried everywhere, and in all manner of vehicles, dashed with ink and wine and rain and tears. A record of a life.

She did not glance at me once, and presently she closed her eyes again.

"Rest," I said, "rest, *ma belle.*"

And she seemed to grow a fraction heavier against me; I was not sure.

All the long panes of the windows were white behind their blinds when Janette came carefully in through the door. I had left it ajar, which had prepared her, but something else had done so, too. Her eyes were bruised, but not from insomnia, her modern garments intangibly askew. She crept towards us, looked down for some moments at the woman I held, and then began to cry.

"She's dead, mademoiselle."

"Yes, Janette."

Camélie's breathing had grown so faint in the last hour I had not heard it stop. Only the feel of that hollow brittle body had subtly altered. Even so, I had not wanted to let her go. Not until, as it were, the final echoes of her soul had died away.

We laid her down, and Janette, business-like but not unkind, wiping her eyes, sent me out. I heard a sound of weighty footsteps in the yard as I went. Jean had already been dispatched for doctor or priest.

I seated myself in the drawing room, cold and still in that white day's beginning. I had better remain. Someone might want to question me. I was not uneasy, nor relieved, nor saddened. I felt the peace of cessation. The loss... This I had suffered long ago.

After about half an hour, I heard men's voices in the yard below, Jean's and another's.

Janette came into the room.

"Don't be alarmed, mademoiselle. There's no – well. We knew it would be just a short while, ever since that day or so ago. A month, maybe, but no more. And likely much less. So we went on, as we always do. Acting cheerfully. The way she wished. She liked happiness round her. She was so sad, but she had been happy once, I am sure. And this is yours, mademoiselle?"

I looked up, and saw she had brought the book.

"No, that is Madame's."

"Madame's *once*," said Janette. "I was with her the day she sold it. There were a lot of things she sold that day. All over the city we went. I was only a shrimp of a thing, and it seemed like a game to me. How I laughed, and Madame laughed too. But this little book, some ancestor wrote the things in it. She was very proud of him, mademoiselle. There's a figure of him in the museum, very handsome, in a sort of top-hat. When she got rid of the book it was as if – as if she tore the very skin of her body to let it free. You may think I exaggerate, but that's how it seemed. The bookshop across the yard – where the wines are now – he had it. Ignorant pig. He paid hardly anything for it." She came towards me, holding out the book, and so I took it, after all.

"Don't be sorry, mademoiselle," said Janette, sobbing. "She was very old. Nearly a hundred, my father says. She'll be glad to be quiet at last."

SEVEN

Where they buried her I have no notion, just as I do not know that communal grave in which Lucien was thrown. The sacraments of death have their value, but it is the living poignant thing which matters. It was here, it is gone. It will come back. The time of live creatures must always be now. So I left her behind me to the care of those who required the solace of that care. And took her with me, too, a part of me, as once before. There are already certain moments in a day, certain nuances of sun-light, a trace of some scent, a particular colour in the sky, on water – which are Camélie. His love, that I remember. His love, and my love. Always, now.

In a sleazy corner shop, amid a heap of tumbled *bric-a-brac*, I sold the lacquer box and each item it contained. I bargained hard and long with the man in his apron. When he called me names, I shrugged them off. I know my role, at last, and it is no longer that of a helpless victim. I will speak out for what I want, and I will, where necessary, fight to get it.

Armoured only in that cliché of destitution, the clothes I stand up in, with just enough money to feed myself or to find haphazard shelter, I am now nerving myself for the final journey, the journey which, once begun, can never end.

Yes, I am afraid of them, the hordes of the city, their sores, their wailing shriek of pain, the head of the cur that snaps about to tear the hand of its rescuer. But the tide, the surging heartbeat of anger, I can feel it too. Like him, I can be given courage by it, and like him, finding a voice, it may be possible to move this stubborn self-perpetuating engine of shame – outward – against the oppressor. Injustice. I have felt the sting of the lash across my spine, my forehead. One lies down beneath the lash or one springs to catch it. What am I saying? I am saying that this mob I fear is built of atoms that are only men, only women, only the multitudes of life of which I, too, am a part. And the howling mob, I am *that* also. Let me howl then. I will not lie down under the lash. I will not let another lie down under it if I can only open their eyes, their minds.

I am not Lucien. But still, I am. And what was left unfinished, festering, is mine to take up again, and so to heal. At least, I may try. I am not Lucien, nor need I die like Lucien. Sometimes the bitterest medicine does the most good. I will remember where the rocks lie and the quicksand. And when to run away, and when to remain.

Today, early, before the steam hells of the laundries on the *Rue George* opened their doors, I went among the women.

I was still afraid of them, but as each one approached, I looked into her eyes and saw, and made her see me in my turn. And before they could press in on me, I reached out to them. Why, they are only muscle and blood and bone, as I am. The smells of gum or unclean flesh are of small importance. Inside each of these wretched cases a spirit and a mind co-exist. Touch these. Without form, without ugliness, without gender, the lamp burns there in everyone.

We spoke a long while, until the clamour of the opening doors summoned them to their chemical inferno. We discussed, almost idly, their non-existent rights, the pittance they are paid, the rotting of their lungs. Each sisterhood is linked by vagrant casual means to the sisterhoods of other laundries, up and down the street, and so with the network of horror-chambers in all the streets around. (Some means to an end here.) There is an idea I may speak more speciously to them, in the gardens by the *Palais-Etoile*, on the next public holiday, which is soon. God knows, I might even pin some green leaves on to my hat for the occasion.

The bright cars thrum on the boulevards. Dream your dream, you chrome dragons. And the tall restaurants inside the palisades of glass, whose doors are more difficult to enter than those of heaven. And the citadel, this too should savour its dream. For there are mice in the basement, sirs. What if they begin to gnaw?

Tonight, I dine on cabbage-stalk soup and sleep on rags or plain boards with the ladies of the *quais*, where it is the rats we shall have to look out for.

Shortly before dusk, I walked beside the river. The air was soft, the pink-blossom sky lay on the water like an opal's blush. I leaned after the sinking light with the book in my hands and read it through. I gazed at the picture Camélie had painted. Long after the day was gone, I found the contours of his face by memory alone. There are a great many bookshops along the *Pré Fevrier*, where the non-monument to La Tour rises like a monstrous headless neck from the trees. Here, wary as a thief, I tucked my book away among the antiquarian manuscripts of some reputable dealer, whose name deliberately I omitted to note.

Someone will find it out one day, maybe divining its worth. Or some other hapless girl-child come across the face of Lucien and fall in love with it. In that instance, love is all it will be.

It pained me to let it go. And I foresee nights of ice and hunger when I shall curse myself that, if I must lose my one treasure, I did not do it for cash. But as Camélie said, some things too precious, too harmful. As for cash, I will recollect the story of the pieces of silver.

It is all done now, all over, the first instalment of the battle. Here I am in the second. If I am to be strong, I do not need the book. For we are one, he and I. The same, complete. Nothing will alter that. *C'est la vérité sans parure.*

And the stars of spring unsheathe themselves like swords.

No, my Lucien, all the candles have not been put out, the night is not dark. Look, there are a thousand candles in the sky above Troy, and in the river, two thousand more.

About the Author

Tanith Lee (1947-2015) was born in London. Because her parents were professional dancers (ballroom, Latin American) and had to live where the work was, she attended a number of truly terrible schools, and didn't learn to read – she was also dyslectic – until almost age 8. And then only because her father taught her. This opened the world of books to her, and by 9 she was writing. After much better education at a grammar school, she went on to work in a library. This was followed by various other jobs – shop assistant, waitress, clerk – plus a year at art college when she was 25-26. In 1974, her career as a writer was launched, when DAW Books of America, under the leadership of Donald A. Wollheim, bought and published *The Birthgrave*, and thereafter 26 of her novels and collections.

Tanith was presented with a Lifetime Achievement Award in 2013, at World Fantasycon in Brighton. During her lifetime, she also received the World Horror Convention Grand Master Award, as well as the August Derleth Award and the World Fantasy Award for short fiction (twice).

In 1992, she married the writer-artist-photographer John Kaiine, her partner since 1987. They lived on the Sussex Weald, near the sea, in a house full of books and plants, and never without feline companions. She died at home in May 2015, after a long illness, continuing to work until a couple of weeks before her death.

Throughout her life, Tanith wrote around 100 books, and over 300 short stories. 4 of her radio plays were broadcast by the BBC; she also wrote 2 episodes (*Sarcophagus* and *Sand*) for the TV series *Blake's 7*. Her stories were read regularly on Radio 4 Extra. She was an inspiration to a generation of writers and her work was enormously influential within genre fiction – as it continues to be. She wrote in many styles, within and across many genres, including Horror, SF and Fantasy, Historical, Detective, Contemporary-Psychological, Children and Young Adult. Her preoccupation, though, was always people.

Books by Tanith Lee

A Selection

The Birthgrave Trilogy (The Birthgrave; Vazkor, son of Vazkor, Quest for
the White Witch)

The Vis Trilogy (The Storm Lord; Anackire; The White Serpent)

The Flat Earth Opus (Night's Master; Death's Master; Delusion's Master;
Delirium's Mistress; Night's Sorceries)

Don't Bite the Sun

Drinking Sapphire Wine

Volkhavaar

The Paradys Quartet (The Book of the Damned; The Book of the Beast; The
Book of the Dead; The Book of the Mad)

The Venus Quartet (Faces Under Water; Saint Fire; A Bed of Earth; Venus
Preserved)

Kill the Dead

Electric Forest

Days of Grass

Sung in Shadow

A Heroine of the World

Sabella

Lycanthia

The Scarabae Blood Opera (Dark Dance; Personal Darkness;
Darkness, I)

The Blood of Roses

When the Lights Go Out

Heart-Beast

Elephantasm

Eva Fairdeath

Reigning Cats and Dogs

Vivia

The Unicorn Trilogy (Black Unicorn; Gold Unicorn; Red Unicorn)

The Claidi Journals (Law of the Wolf Tower; Wolf Star Rise, Queen of the
Wolves, Wolf Wing)

The Piratica Novels (Piratica 1; Piratica 2; Piratica 3)

The Silver Metal Lover

Metallic Love

Death of the Day

The Gods Are Thirsty

Mortal Suns

The Lionwolf Trilogy (Cast a Bright Shadow, Here in Cold Hell, No Flame but Mine)

Collections

Nightshades
Dreams of Dark and Light
Women as Demons
Red as Blood – Tales from the Sisters Grimmer
Tamastara, or the Indian Nights
The Gorgon
Tempting the Gods
Hunting the Shadows
Sounds and Furies
Dancing in the Fire
Colder Greyer Stones
Space is Just a Starry Night
Phantasya
Blood 20

Also Published by Immanion Press

The Colouring Book Series
Greyglass
To Indigo
L'Amber
Killing Violets
Ivoria
Cruel Pink
Turquoiselle

Ghosteria Volume 1: The Stories
Ghosteria Volume 2: The Novel: Zircons May Be Mistaken
A Different City
Legenda Maris
Animate Objects
The Weird Tales of Tanith Lee

IMMANION PRESS
Purveyors of Speculative Fiction

34 by Tanith Lee (writing as Esther Garber)

Tanith Lee 'co-wrote' *34* with Esther Garber – a fictional character (perhaps?). This is Esther's autobiography – but how much of it is true? Are her recollections of her unusual childhood in Egypt correct? And what of the mysterious 'gentleman', who Esther meets in France after having run away from home, who initiates her into forbidden pleasures of a Sapphic kind? Is she haunted or merely manipulated? Is she in love or simply obsessed? After one night of passion, Esther pursues her elusive tormentor into what seems to be a fairy-tale version of the French countryside, to journey's end and revelation, but also further mystery. Sensual, thought-provoking, and with an unreliable narrator, who twists and turns within her own tortured story, *34* demonstrates that haunting comes in many forms. As does desire. This new edition also includes the author's essay, on her work with Esther and Judas Garber: 'Meeting the Garbers'. ISBN: 978-1-907737-82-4 £10.99 $13.99

A Raven Bound with Lilies by Storm Constantine

Androgynous, and stronger in mind and body than humans, naturally magical, sometimes deadly, and often possessing unearthly beauty, the Wraeththu have captivated readers since Storm Constantine's first novel, *The Enchantments of Flesh and Spirit*, was published in 1988, regarded as ground-breaking in its treatment of gender and sexuality. This anthology of 15 tales collects all her published Wraeththu short stories into one volume, and also includes extra material. The tales range from the 'creation story' *Paragenesis*, through the bloody, brutal rise of the earliest tribes, and on into a future, where strange mutations are starting to emerge from hidden corners of the earth. With sumptuous illustrations by official Wraeththu artist Ruby, *A Raven Bound with Lilies* is a must for any Wraeththu enthusiast, and is also a comprehensive introduction to the mythos for those who are new to it. ISBN: 978-1-907737-80-0 £11.99, $15.50

http://www.immanion-press.com
info@immanion-press.com

www.newconpress.co.uk/

Tanith By Choice
Tanith Lee

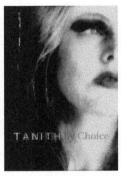

Tanith Lee is one of the finest writers ever to grace the field of speculative fiction. The author of around 100 novels and several hundred short stories, she wrote two episodes of the iconic TV series *Blake's 7*, was the first woman to win the British Fantasy Award – which she followed with two World Fantasy Awards, shortlistings for all manner of accolades including Nebula and BSFA Awards – and in 2013 she received a 'Lifetime Achievement Award' from the organisers of World Fantasycon…

"Tanith has left one heck of a legacy. I would never dream of attempting to compile a 'Best of' collection, so instead I've let others do so for me."

– editor Ian Whates

Tanith By Choice features many of her finest stories, as chosen by those who knew her. With contributions from **Storm Constantine, Craig Gidney, Mavis Haut, Stephen Jones, John Kaiine** (Tanith's widower), **Vera Nazarian, Sarah Singleton, Kari Sperring, Sam Stone, Cecilia Dart-Thornton, Freda Warrington**, and **Ian Whates**, each story is accompanied by a note from the person responsible for selecting it explaining why this tale means so much to them.

Released September 2017. Available as a paperback and a numbered, limited edition hardback.

www.newconpress.co.uk